Please Don't Eat Me

Liz Climo

LB
Little, Brown and Company
NEW YORK BOSTON

Ooh!

Aw, nuts.

Please don't eat me.
But I'm so hungry.
Okay, I'll order you a pizza.

So, can I have the last slice?
Not unless you want me to eat you.

Okay, Bear. I got you a pizza. You aren't gonna eat me now, right?

I don't know.... It just doesn't feel like a meal without dessert.

Okay, bye.

Wait! I still need to eat you! My friends will make fun of me if I don't.

Oh...no. I am being eaten. What a bummer. Ouch.

Okay, are we good now?
Oh, those guys weren't my friends.

looking good, man!

Now I'm leaving.
Can I have your foot first? I hear a rabbit's foot is lucky.

Uh...

Here you go! This is even *luckier* than a rabbit's foot! It's, like, *way* luckier. A rabbit's foot isn't even lucky. No way, not one bit.
Okay, toodle-oo!

Wait—are you sure I shouldn't eat you? I mean, you *did* burrow through my lawn earlier. That was pretty rude.

For crying out loud.

DO
This
means

DO
NOT
BURROW
This
means
you,
bunnies

Grass
Seed

Okay, see ya.

Wait...

Fine.
That's it!
Just eat me
already!

STOMP
STOMP
STOMP

I don't want
to eat you.
I like you.

Are you kidding? Then why did you put me through all of that?

I didn't want you to leave. I like hanging out with you.
I don't have many friends.
And besides, didn't we have fun?

Yeah, I suppose we did.

So...
what should we do now?

Well...
I AM starting to get a little hungry....

Aw, nuts.